SARAH LEAN's fascination with animals began
when she was aged eight and a stray cat walked
in the back door and decided to adopt her.
As a child she wanted to be a writer and used
to dictate stories to her mother, until she bought
a laptop of her own several years ago and decided
to type them herself. She loves her garden, art,
calligraphy and spending time outdoors. She lives
in Dorset and shares the space around her desk
with her dogs, Harry and Coco.

Also by Sarah Lean

For older readers:

A Dog Called Homeless

A Horse for Angel

The Forever Whale

Jack Pepper

Hero

Harry and Hope

TIGER DAYS

and the secret cat

SARAH LEAN

Illustrations by Anna Currey

HarperCollins *Children's Books*

First published in Great Britain by HarperCollins *Children's Books* in 2016
HarperCollins *Children's Books* is a division of HarperCollins*Publishers* Ltd,
1 London Bridge Street, London, SE1 9GF

The HarperCollins website address is: www.harpercollins.co.uk

1

Text © Sarah Lean 2016
Illustrations © Anna Currey 2016

ISBN 978-00-0-816566-6

Sarah Lean asserts the moral right to be identified as the author of the work.
Anna Currey asserts the moral right to be identified as the illustrator of the work.

Printed and bound in England by Clays Ltd, St Ives plc

MIX
**Paper from
responsible sources**

FSC˚ C007454

FSC™ is a non-profit international organisation established to promote
the responsible management of the world's forests. Products carrying the
FSC label are independently certified to assure consumers that they come
from forests that are managed to meet the social, economic and
ecological needs of present and future generations,
and other controlled sources.

Find out more about HarperCollins and the environment at
www.harpercollins.co.uk/green

*To Fallon, one of the
bravest I ever met*

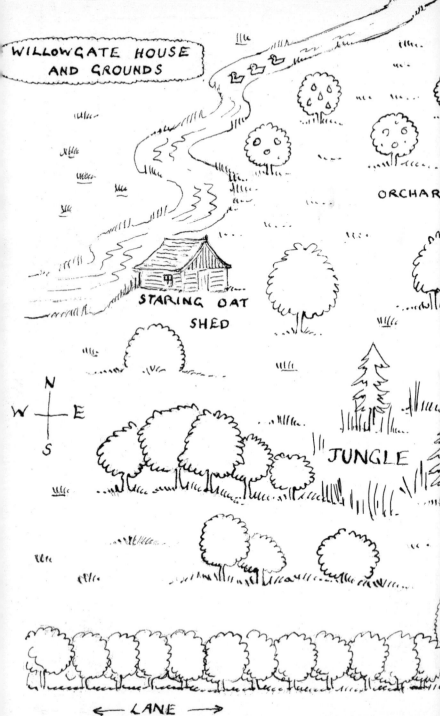

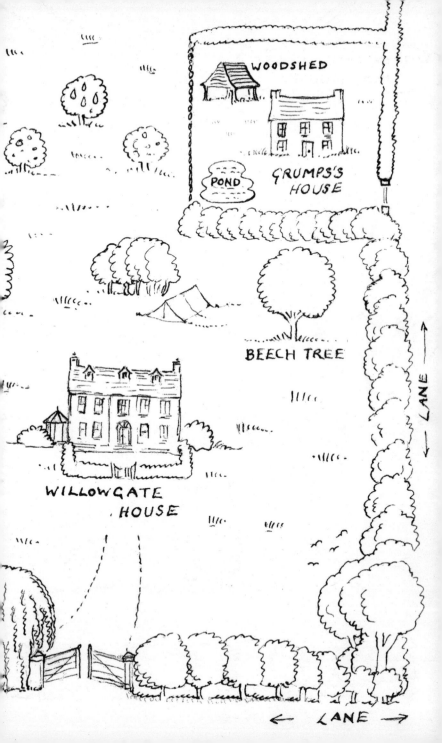

Chapter 1

Tiger's Bedroom

Tiger Days didn't know anyone who loved tigers as much as she did.

She wore tiger pyjamas, socks and slippers, and spent a lot of time in her bedroom reading about tigers and drawing tiger pictures. Her parents would often suggest bike rides and trips to the swimming pool on Saturday afternoons, but Tiger would much rather be in her bedroom doing tiger things.

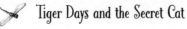

One Saturday afternoon, her parents appeared at her door.

"You'll never guess who that was on the phone…" said Mum.

"Hmmmm?" said Tiger, not really listening.

Dad rolled his eyes as Tiger's nose stayed firmly buried in her wildlife book. "It was May Days!" he said.

Tiger looked up, surprised. May Days was her grandmother and had been living in Africa on a wildlife reserve since Tiger was a baby. Whenever May Days phoned, Tiger asked when she was coming to visit, but May Days said it was hard to know because the giraffes or rhinos always needed her more.

This time, May Days had phoned with wonderful news. She had finally come back to England and bought a place called Willowgate House.

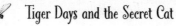

"She wants you to go and stay," said Dad. "You can have your first adventure together at the new house."

Tiger wrinkled her nose. She was sometimes nervous about doing new things and the idea of a real-life adventure with May Days was a little scary. She had a feeling May Days wasn't going to be like everyone else's grandmother.

"Won't you be worried about me?" she asked her parents.

"While you're with May Days? Not even for a second," said Mum, although it was obvious that *somebody* was worried.

But Tiger put on a brave smile for her

parents. An adventure with May Days
would be great, wouldn't it?

"Are you sure this is the right house?" said
Tiger.

She stood close to her dad by the gate,
beneath a large drooping willow tree.

Willowgate House was unexpectedly
huge, and it stood at the end of a long
driveway. It had wide windows and tall
chimney pots, and a conservatory that
leaned slightly to the left.

Tiger tilted her head to the side to see if
it looked any straighter. But it didn't. The
lopsided building made her feel wobbly.

Tiger waited on the doorstep behind Dad while he pulled the bell on the wall beside the door.

The next surprise was May Days.

Weren't grandmothers supposed to be old and grey and worn?

Instead she had curls that were wild and alive. Her sleeves were pushed up, as if she'd done a hard day's work, and she bounded out like the kind of person who didn't sit down very often.

"You're here, at last!" May Days beamed, throwing her arms around Dad first, and then around Tiger. Tiger peered behind her grandmother at the bare floorboards and curved staircase in

the hall. It looked as if nobody had lived
here for a very long time.

"You were no bigger than a koala
the last time I saw you," May Days said,

holding Tiger by the cheeks. Tiger blinked
in surprise, and her tummy did a flip.

"You've got a big house," said Tiger,
not sure what else to say.

"Too big for one person," May
Days said, chuckling like a barrel full of
chickens. "Come in! Come in!"

Mr Days had also not seen his mother
for a very long time and he had lots to
tell her over gallons of tea. They laughed
and talked while Tiger sat on a chair, still
clinging to her tiger-striped suitcase. The
faded lino flooring curled up in the corners
of the kitchen, and there wasn't a lot more

to see than an old cooking range and a
long pine table that had worn into a curve
in the middle. Where were the proper
kitchen cupboards and worktops? Tiger
hoped that the rest of the house had been
decorated.

"Thank you for bringing me my
granddaughter," May Days said,
squeezing Mr Days' cheeks when he had
to leave.

Tiger clung to her dad for an extra-long
hug.

"Are you sure you don't need me at
home?" Tiger whispered.

"We'll miss you terribly," said Mr
Days, "but you and your grandmother

have a lot of catching up to do."

"It's just you and me," said May Days, after they'd waved the car into the distance.

"Shall I put my things in my room?" said Tiger.

"Your room?" said May Days, smiling. "You'd better come with me."

May Days showed Tiger the outside bathroom first. Although the walls and floor were bare brick, there were soft towels, a cup for toothbrushes, a mirror and a light bulb with a long pull cord, all sparkling clean. Tiger tried to smile brightly.

"I'm afraid we haven't got a shower or bath yet," said May Days. "But I have spare flannels if you need one."

She turned Tiger's shoulders to face
the back garden. "We're going to share a
room."

Tiger would have her own room one
day, May Days assured her, but all of
Willowgate needed a lot of work first.

For now, they were going to be staying in the garden in an old green tent.

A tent? thought Tiger, her eyes wide. *Outside?!*

Chapter 2

An Extra Guest

Tiger sat on one side of the long kitchen table and drew a tiger. She kept her pens tidy and was colouring carefully.

"Do you know what my favourite animal is?" Tiger asked May Days.

"A tapir?" May Days smiled.

"No." Tiger scratched her head. "Even though I don't know what that is."

Tiger stretched her arms as wide as

they would go. "It's bigger than my arms, and about this high." She measured a level beyond her head and thought for a moment.

"Maybe a bit bigger or smaller, I can't tell when I'm sitting down. And it's black and white—"

"A panda?" said May Days.

"And orange."

"An orang-utan?" May Days chuckled. "An orange bear?"

Tiger squinted, because she wasn't sure if May Days was joking, and held up the picture she was drawing for her.

"Oh!" said May Days, as if she'd suddenly remembered. "I know what it is! Did you know that I adore tigers too?"

Just then a horn honked loudly outside and made Tiger jump and colour over the lines.

"I expect that's my other guest," said May Days, which made Tiger's tummy turn higgledy-piggledy again. Nobody had said anything to Tiger about anyone else coming to stay.

A van had pulled up beside the house, and a young man wearing a green

boilersuit and dark sunglasses jumped out
of the driver's seat.

"You must be Tiger," said the man.
"I've heard how ferocious you are." He
grinned, but Tiger wasn't sure what he
meant.

"This is Dennis," said May Days.
"He's escaped from the zoo, and cheeky
as a monkey."

But it wasn't Dennis that would be
staying at Willowgate.

They all went around to the back
of the van and Tiger's mouth fell open.
There, inside, huddled in a cage in the
straw, was a snout-nosed, tippy-toed,
bristled, sorry-looking, saggy-skinned…

"What is it?" said Tiger, pulling a confused face.

"A warthog," said Dennis. "Known to us zookeepers as a wartie. Don't you just love her?"

The warthog was knobbly and brown and Tiger did not like the look of it at all.

The warthog was the other guest.

Being so young and small, the warthog would be kept in a pen in the kitchen and was going to need a lot of attention. Dennis clipped four meshed panels together to make the sides of a pen, and bundled in some straw. The little warthog sat in the middle and shook. From the other side of the room Tiger shuddered and sat back

at the kitchen table, while
May Days got the warthog
out of the pen, put a
towel on her lap and
fed the wrinkly
little creature
from a baby's
bottle. The
warthog guzzled and
milk dribbled down its chin.

"Would you like to feed her?" asked May
Days, but Tiger was busy drawing again.

"Would you like to hold her?" asked
May Days, but Tiger had colouring to
finish.

"Would you like to give her a name?"

said May Days, and Tiger looked up and said she'd think about that.

Tiger thought of Stinky and Saggy, Snorty and Pooper, but none of these names seemed to quite sum up the knockedy-kneed creature. She'd have to think some more, but it was hard to find a name for something she didn't really care for.

Dennis sat at the table beside Tiger and told her what he did at the zoo. It was mostly feeding and cleaning poop by the sound of it, but he did look very interesting in his dark glasses, with his wide smile, and Tiger thought she might prefer it if Dennis was staying instead of the warthog.

"Isn't Willowgate amazing?" asked Dennis.

Tiger put the lid back on her orange colouring pen. She'd finished a tiger picture for Dennis too, but neither of the drawings made her feel happy like she did in her room at home.

Tiger thought about home, her family, her soft bed, her striped blanket and the sign on her bedroom door with her name on it.

"I've never been to a house where a warthog lived in the kitchen. And I've never camped in a tent," Tiger said, quietly.

"I don't suppose it feels like home to the wartie yet either," said Dennis. The wartie was back in the pen, her head drooping.

"What was her old home like?" said Tiger.

"Empty," he said. "She's an orphan."

Tiger leaned over the table. The warthog looked up. Tiny dark eyes glistened and blinked at Tiger. That's why she looked so sad. She had no family anywhere at all.

"Hello," said Tiger to the wartie, even though they had already met.

"Are you missing home?" asked May Days that night when Tiger was zipped up in her sleeping bag on her camp bed.

"Yes," she said. "Do you miss Africa?"

"Terribly," May Days said. "Makes me feel all out of sorts."

Tiger whispered, "I know what you mean. Being here feels a bit unusual and skew-whiff in your tummy."

"We'll be fine," said May Days, and they held hands across the tent. "Have you thought of a name for the wartie yet?"

Tiger nodded. "Monday," she said.

"I like it," said May Days. "What made you think of that?"

"Because Monday is the beginning of the week, and being here is the beginning of something new," said Tiger, softly. "And as we are all Days I thought she might like to be part of our family too."

Chapter 3

What's That Strange Noise?

Tiger was used to the bustling and rumbling of cars, buses and trains in the town where she lived, but there were more unusual sounds at Willowgate.

"What's that screeching?" Tiger asked.

"A barn owl," said May Days.

"What's that plopping?" Tiger asked.

"Squirrels dropping pine cones on the roof."

"What's that racket?" Tiger said in the

kitchen one day.

"Oh dear," May Days said as the ceiling shuddered and the pipes grumbled. "The plumbing's up the spout."

The perilous plumbing filled the old house with a hullabaloo whenever a tap was turned on, so May Days called a plumber. When he arrived, May Days helped him to pull up floorboards to fix the plunking pipes.

"What is that other strange noise?" Tiger said, hearing a yowling sound. "Is there another creature in the house?"

Monday the wartie stood up in her pen and pricked her ears.

Tiger didn't want to investigate the

strange noise by herself, so instead went
outside, sat in the tent and put a blanket
over her head.

"Hello!" a voice said from outside
the tent.

"Who's there?" Tiger said.

"Tom Henry Thomas," replied the
voice. "Who are you?"

"Tiger," she said, peeping outside
the tent. But she couldn't see anyone…
Hearing a gasp, she quickly added, "I'm
not an actual tiger, it's just my name.
Where are you?"

"In the hedge," said the voice and a
boy poked his head out of the leaves and
crawled forward on his hands and knees.

"Could the noise be the sound of a despicabor?" he said.

Tiger giggled. "What's a despicabor?"

"I don't know," Tom said. "I made it up. Grumps says I've got a livid imagination. I'm staying at his house next door."

"I'd like to know what's making the noise, but I don't want to find out by myself. It might just be a mouse, but it

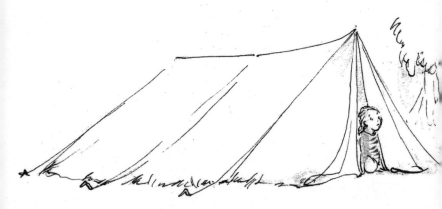

might be something scarier…" Tiger said.

"I'll come with you!" Tom said
enthusiastically. "Wait for me. I'll be back
in a minute."

Tom crawled back through the hedge
and returned a minute later with a wire
cage the size of a small shoe box and
a piece of cheese, just in case it was a
mouse.

Tom's grandfather, Grumps, had mice in his woodshed. He'd catch them in the trap and let them go in the fields.

Tom and Tiger went around to the front of Willowgate House, through the hall, and slowly crept up the stairs. They couldn't hear the yowling sound any more, but it had seemed like it was coming from upstairs.

The floorboards along the hallway groaned like old bones.

"It didn't sound like *that*, did it?" Tom said.

"Not really," said Tiger.

They pushed the first door open and peered into the bathroom. Orange rust crackled the bottom of the bath and fungus grew on the wall.

"Zombie mushrooms," Tom whispered in a dreaded, doomed kind of way.

"I don't think mushrooms can make noises," Tiger said.

They turned a bath tap each. The taps coughed and spluttered, the pipes clanged. Tiger shook her head. It wasn't any of those sounds either.

Tiger and Tom crept close to the wall and crouched behind the last door in the hallway. They closed one eye each and peeped through the gap between the door and the wall. They couldn't see anything, but it seemed just as good a place as any to set the trap.

With a hunk of cheese inside and the trapdoor caught open on a spring, they crept away and waited halfway down the stairs.

"We actually had a school pet mouse," whispered Tiger.

"Did you look after it?" said Tom.

"No, I'm the pencil monitor," Tiger said. "I keep all the pencils sharp, which is tricky when some people chew both ends."

Snap! The trap clapped shut and Tiger followed Tom, holding on to the edge of his T-shirt.

There was nothing in the trap except the cheese, but the door of the cupboard in the hallway was now open a little.

Something moved inside.

Tom crept over and looked back at Tiger. She gulped and said, "One, two, three!"

Tom flung open the door.

"Yeeowwrrreeeeow!" said the creature inside, giving them a fright. Tiger jumped and Tom slammed the cupboard shut.

They galloped down the stairs and raced to the kitchen.

"What was it?!" said Tiger.

Tom skidded to a halt. "I didn't see, but could it be one of those?" he said, pointing at the bristly creature jumping up at the pen.

"That's Monday, our wartie, but we've only got one," Tiger said.

Tom was still pointing. "What did you say it was?"

"A warthog," said Tiger. "Listen!"

There was the strange yowling noise again, this time sounding as though it was coming from the wall... Monday stood still, her ears up, her tail stiff like a flag.

Her nose twitched towards a cupboard
in the corner of the kitchen, directly below
the one upstairs.

Tiger and Tom tiptoed over. They
counted to three again and then threw
open the door. Inside was empty, but there
was a hole halfway up the wall, with
ropes hanging straight down. Tom pulled
the rope a little.

"It's a lift to the upstairs cupboard,"
said Tiger, as the shelf lowered.

"A very small lift," said Tom,
wondering what it was for. "But if the
mystery creature is inside…"

"It will come down with it!" finished
Tiger, her eyes popping wide.

"You've got a warthog in your kitchen," Tom said slowly. "That means there could be anything in the lift."

"Whatever it is, it might be trapped, so we have to rescue it. You pull the rope, Tom. I'll stand over there and keep guard."

Monday looked exceptionally keen to find out too.

Tom took a deep breath and tugged on the rope. The pulley was stiff and creaked, but Tom heaved and pulled until the bottom edge of the lift appeared. One more big pull and…

The lift shot down with a bump and Tom dived behind the table with Tiger.

"Yeeowwrrreeeeow!" said a voice from the lift.

Monday squealed back.

Tiger put her hands over her eyes, while Tom quickly peeped over the top of a chair. He caught only a glimpse of the mystery creature before he slid back down to the floor.

"Well?" Tiger said. "Is it strange or scary?"

Before Tom could answer, the mystery creature had already jumped out of the lift and headed over to the children.

It hooked its tail around the chair leg. "Rowwrrreeeeow," it said, peering round at the children.

49

"Arrgghhh!" shrieked Tom, pulling the front of his T-shirt over his head.

"Tom," Tiger said calmly, "it's just a cat."

The cat looked Tiger up and down, put her nose in the air and sauntered away. Just a cat!

The children tried to follow the white cat with the softly weaving tail and to tempt her with a saucer of milk, while Monday sulked alone in her pen. But no matter what the children did, the cat wouldn't come over to them. She turned away, twitched her tail, and padded back upstairs.

She seemed quite at home at Willowgate, though.

"What was that strange yowling noise earlier today?" May Days said in the tent that night.

"A mystery cat," Tiger smiled. "She

51

lives in the house and so does a warthog, but we have to live in a tent outside."

May Days chuckled.

"It is very skew-whiff here," Tiger said.

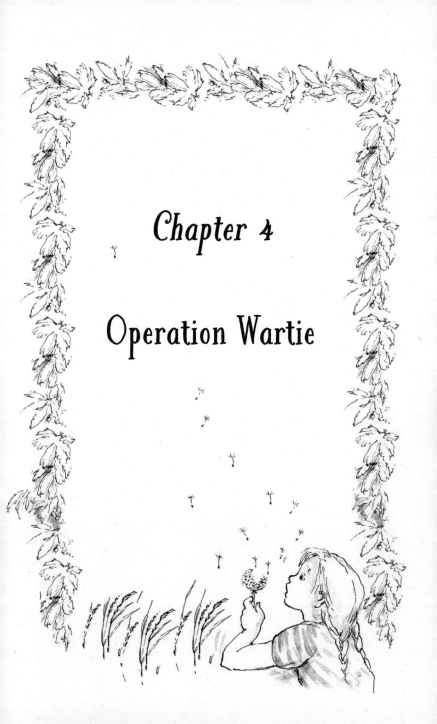

Chapter 4

Operation Wartie

The perilous plumbing was underway.
May Days was still assisting the
plumber and had little time to look after
Monday.

Whenever May Days needed help to
feed the wartie or clean the pen, Tiger had
an excuse – a picture to colour, a chapter
in her book to read, or a letter to write
to Mum and Dad. Tiger wanted to help
May Days, but the thought of cleaning

up poopy straw and having to hold a scratchy, wriggling wartie didn't sound like fun. Besides, Tiger wouldn't know what to do…

"I wonder who's brave enough to train a warthog?" said May Days.

Train a warthog? That sounded a lot more appealing than feeding and cleaning.

"What will this brave person have to do?" Tiger said, looking up from her half-coloured tiger picture.

"Follow some instructions," May Days said, waving a list. She yawned. She'd been up several times in the night to comfort Monday, who whined and squealed at being left on her own in the kitchen.

Tiger twitched her mouth from side to side. "I'll go and get Tom."

Tiger ran to the hole under the hedge, but instead of finding Tom, there was a clean empty tin can lying there. A long piece of string disappeared through the hedge and a rolled note was inside the tin. It said:

Dear Tiger,

This is a Tin-a-phone. If you pull the string tight and speak loudly into the tin, I can hear you. If you put it over your ear, you can hear me. I'm waiting in my bedroom. I've got a tin on the other end.

From Tom Henry Thomas.

P.S. Pull the string tight.

Tiger pulled the string and felt it go taut.

"Hello, Tom? Are you there?" she said and then held the tin next to her ear.

A tinny little voice came back, "I can hear you, Tiger! You have to say 'over' when you finish speaking. Over."

"OK. Over," Tiger said.

"Also, when you begin, you have to say: 'Tom, this is Tiger' and then say your message. Over."

"Tom, this is Tiger. Please can you come round for Operation Wartie. Over."

"Tiger, this is Tom. Yes, I can come over. Over. Oh, that sounded funny because I said 'over' twice... Over." Tom groaned.

The string went slack, and a moment later Tom crawled through the hedge.

"What's Operation Wartie?" he said eagerly.

"Only for the brave," Tiger said. "We're going to train a warthog."

Tom grinned.

Tiger turned back towards the house and saw the mysterious white cat watching them from a window upstairs.

"Hello, cat," Tiger called, as she didn't have a name for her yet. "It's Operation Wartie today. You can come if you like?" But the cat turned her marble eyes away.

The first instruction from May Days said this:

1. Monday needs to learn to drink from a dish instead of a bottle.

Tiger weighed and mixed together Monday's drink, which consisted of soya milk, a white powder from the vet and porridge. Tiger passed the dish to Tom, who climbed on a chair and into the pen. He kneeled and carefully lowered the dish to the ground. Monday trotted over and straight away stuck her nose in the mixture. She snorted and sneezed froth all over Tom, which made them laugh.

"Has she actually drunk anything?" said Tiger.

Tom shrugged. "Most of it is up her nose or on the floor."

"Let's see what the next instruction is," said Tiger. Perhaps there was something easier to do.

2. Dig a den – see Wild Lives book.

May Days had left a book open with a sentence underlined in pencil. She had also drawn a small map of the garden, and marked where the den should be, between the tent and the beech tree.

"*Warthogs often sleep in abandoned*

aardvark dens," Tiger read from the book. "*They use their snouts to dig…* Is a snout the same as a nose, Tom?"

"I think so," he said, wriggling his nostrils.

"Does that mean we have to dig with our noses?"

Tom pointed to the two spades leaning by the back door.

"Phew!" said Tiger. But she'd never used a spade before. At home Mum had a trowel for the plant pots, and Dad had a hose pipe to clean the patio, but they didn't have a lawn or spades.

There was only one thing for it…

"Come on, Tom," said Tiger, picking up

a spade and heading out to the garden.

The ground beneath the beech tree was hard and the spade swayed when Tiger stood on it. Tom and Tiger made lots of narrow dips in the earth with the spades, but the swaying was so much fun that they forgot what they were supposed to be doing, until they noticed the cat sitting nearby.

"The cat wants to learn how to make a den too," laughed Tom.

As if she knew she was being talked about, the cat twitched her tail in the air and strolled away.

"Do you think Monday should be watching us dig so she can learn?" said Tiger.

"Good idea!" said Tom and they raced back to the kitchen.

Tiger asked Tom to bring the warthog, and he carried her at arm's length as she wriggled excitedly in his hands. Tiger dragged the pen across the kitchen, laughing as she bumped into the table and chairs and down the kitchen doorstep. Eventually she reached the beech tree and gently rested the pen on the ground and Tom put Monday back inside.

"Pay attention, Monday," said Tiger. "We're going to teach you how to dig a den."

Tiger and Tom tried to dig again, but after a few minutes they were worn out and Monday was hanging her head, whining unhappily.

"Do you think Monday is still hungry?" said Tiger.

They decided to take her back to the kitchen to try feeding her again, but the second time was no better than the first – bubbles, snorts and a bottom in the dish.

Tiger didn't know what to do so she sat on the floor of the pen and sighed. May Days came into the kitchen. "How are you getting on?" she said.

Tiger buried her head in her arms and Tom flopped in a chair.

"We have been extremely unsuccessful at being warthog trainers," said Tiger.

"We couldn't even do number one."

Tiger kept her head buried and pointed to the oats and milk, spilled and splattered, and to the straw and mud spread to the open back door.

"It was too hard," wailed Tiger, and Monday whined again.

May Days' face still glowed with Africa's sunshine and from something warm inside herself.

"If somebody else is brave enough to train the wartie tomorrow," said May Days, "what advice shall we give them?"

Tiger and Tom had lots of answers for this: Don't put Monday's drink in a dish that's bigger than her. Don't sway on the spade if digging is too hard. Learn how to dig!

May Days said this would be very helpful advice, but Monday was hungry and needed feeding now. She made up a bottle of milk and fed her with that instead.

"I wasn't expecting you to train her all in one day," said May Days, "but who has been brave enough to begin to try to train a wartie?" The children smiled at each other. "And, more importantly, who learned something along the way?"

Tiger climbed out of the pen, so relieved, and hugged her grandmother around her middle. "We have," said Tiger.

"And one more thing," said May Days.

"I heard rather a lot of giggling today. Somebody must have been having fun along the way."

"Do you want to try again tomorrow, Tom?" said Tiger.

Of course he did.

That night May Days cupped her hands. She held something invisible and passed it to Tiger to put in her pocket.

"It's only small," she said, "but even the smallest thing can be very valuable."

"What is it?" said Tiger.

"A little Tiger Bravery. And you definitely earned it today."

Chapter 5

Operation Cat

The white cat came and went at Willowgate as if she owned the place. She would slink through the open front door and then saunter out the back, and sometimes she could be found sitting in the lift in the wall.

May Days had explained to Tiger that the lift was used in the olden days for taking hot dinners upstairs, so the butlers and maids didn't trip on the stairs and spill the gravy.

"Why did they take the dinner upstairs?" Tiger asked.

"Because the dining room was upstairs."

"It's always been skew-whiff here," Tiger said, although that gave her an idea about how to train Monday, with the cat's help...

Dennis the zookeeper regularly called at Willowgate to see how the warthog was getting along. Monday had to be measured and weighed to make sure she was eating enough and growing.

Tiger saw Dennis's van driving

towards Willowgate, so she ran down the drive to open the gate for him. She climbed in the passenger seat for a lift back up to the house.

"How do you train a cat?" Tiger asked Dennis.

"If we're talking about big cats, like lions," Dennis said, "I'd say keep well away from sharp claws and teeth, and remember they're smart when they're hungry."

"What about small white ones?" said Tiger.

"Hmmm," Dennis scratched his chin. "I'd probably say the same."

Dennis had brought a package and a tin bucket.

"What are they for?" said Tiger.

"For you and Tom," said Dennis. "I heard you were planning on becoming animal trainers." Dennis explained how the bucket was his secret weapon when it came to training.

Tiger opened the parcel on the kitchen table and then ran to the hedge, tugging at the string on the Tin-a-phone until she felt it go taut at the other end.

"Tom, this is Tiger. You'd better get over here quick. I'm so excited! Today is Operation Cat. Over."

"Yippee!" shrieked Tom. "Over."

Dennis had brought the bucket to help with training, but he'd also brought

Tom and Tiger something to help them feel more like animal trainers – green boilersuits and sunglasses, just like his! The clothes were the smallest he could find, although still a little on the loose side. May Days snipped off part of the arms and legs, rolled up the ragged ends and tied their waists with belts. Tiger and Tom put on their dark sunglasses and felt very interesting and professional indeed.

"Operation Cat has begun," said Tom boldly.

The white cat had come into the kitchen to see what was going on, her tail weaving like a cobra.

"Cat, we'd like your help," said Tiger,

but the haughty white cat strolled away

and went back upstairs. "Don't worry,

Tom," said Tiger. "That is part of the plan." And she told him what they needed to do.

"But what's the bucket for?" asked Tom.

"It's a surprise, but you'll find out soon!" said Tiger.

The children collected lots of small bowls and saucers from the kitchen shelf. They put a small spoonful of warthog milky mixture in half of them, and a spoonful of cat food in the other half.

Tiger put a milk bowl in Monday's pen and a saucer of cat food in the lift. While she banged the tin bucket with a spoon, Tom hauled the lift upstairs. They listened for the soft thud of paws going into the lift and then, a minute later, jumping out again. They lowered the lift back down.

The saucer was empty. The cat had eaten the food.

Monday tried to sit in her food bowl, but it was too small and she knocked it over, but no animal trainer minded that.

Every now and again Tiger gave

Monday another bowl of milk and banged the bucket while Tom hauled more cat food upstairs. Monday tried kneeling in her food, sitting in it, sticking her head in it, but she didn't know how to drink it.

And then, just as they were about to give up, Tom lowered the lift down and the cat was inside.

Tiger and Tom giggled. This is exactly what they had hoped would happen.

The cat looked up and licked her chops, as though she wasn't the slightest bit bothered about what was going on. Monday quivered with excitement at seeing the cat appear in the wall.

Tiger put a saucer of milk on the floor next to the pen and a new bowl of milky mixture inside the pen for Monday, then she banged the bucket again.

 81

Tiger tugged Tom's sleeve and they crept out the back door and crouched underneath the kitchen window. They slowly stood up to peek through the window and saw the cat jump down from the lift.

Tiger and Tom held their breath in anticipation.

The cat walked over, sat down beside the pen and lapped at the saucer of milk. Monday pushed her nose through a gap, trying to sniff the cat and then she looked long and hard at the creature drinking her milk. Monday looked at her own bowl and then back at the cat. Suddenly Monday knelt down on her knobbly knees and slurped from her own bowl, copying the cat.

Tiger and Tom leapt up like kangaroos. "We did it!" said Tiger.

"We are real animal trainers now!" said Tom. "But I still don't understand why you had to bang the bucket?"

"It's a zookeeper's secret weapon," said Tiger. "Every time you bang the bucket they know they're going to get food. They're smartest and learn best when they're hungry. Dennis taught me that."

"Tom! Tom!" his grandfather was calling through the hedge. "Dinner time!"

"Grumps," Tiger heard Tom say as he crawled home through the hedge, "what you could actually do is bang a bucket instead of shouting, and I'll know it's dinner time."

Tiger was still smiling at the end of the day.

"Today you taught Monday how to drink from a bowl," May Days said, kissing her goodnight. "Now all you have to do is teach her to dig a den."

Tiger snuggled into her sleeping bag and May Days turned out the lamp.

"Today I also thought of a good name for that mysterious white cat," whispered Tiger. "Can we call her Holly?"

"Is that because her sharp claws are like a prickly bush?" said May Days.

"No, because I hope she will always be

here when I come to stay in the holidays."

May Days began to chuckle and Tiger giggled.

From now on, Holly Days would be part of the family too.

Chapter 6

Mud and Us

The orphan warthog was an escape artist.

Monday was getting bigger and stronger. Whenever she was left alone for too long, she jumped up against the side of the pen, knocked it over and escaped, and Tiger would have to herd her back.

Dennis came over to weigh the warthog again and was very pleased with her ballooning belly.

Monday could now feed from the bowl, but she still had a lot to learn about being a warthog.

"Some things happen naturally," said Dennis, "and for other things she'll need a helping hand. Who's got helping hands?"

"Us!" said Tiger and Tom, turning over their palms.

Dennis showed Tiger and Tom the correct way to dig and helped them start the den in the shadow of the beech tree, before he left to go back to the zoo. Tiger rolled up her sleeves and tied up her hair, enjoying the new experience of digging and feeling strong and useful.

When the den was just about complete,

Tom noticed the Tin-a-phone jiggling by the hedge and they both ran over to pull it tight and pressed their ears against the tin.

"Hello?" said Tom, not sure who it could be. "This is Tom and Tiger's Tin-a-phone. Who's there? Over."

"Hello? This is Grumps. I've made some limeade and coconut biscuits and I wondered if you could think of anyone I could invite to share them with. Over."

"This is Tom," said Tom into the Tin-a-phone. "I don't know anyone around here. Over."

91

Tiger tapped Tom on the shoulder and took the tin from him. "This is Tiger speaking. I can think of someone. Over."

"Who might that be? Over," said Grumps.

"Us!" giggled Tiger.

Grumps's laughter made a lovely clanging sound, echoing through the tin.

"I say," said Grumps, beaming at the children in their zookeeper outfits, "you must be Tiger, the animal expert."

Tiger blushed, but was very pleased to hear that.

"You must be... is Grumps actually

your name?" said Tiger.

"Tom calls me Grumps because he says I'm grumpy," he laughed.

"It's our family joke," said Tom, "like when you call a tall person shorty."

Tiger and Tom lay on a picnic rug beside Grumps's pond and in the warmth of the contented afternoon Grumps soon fell asleep in his deckchair.

Frogs' eyes poked through the surface of the pond like bubbles. Dragonflies buzzed past Tiger and Tom's ears, like soft electricity, and bees burbled on the buddleia bush.

It had been hard work digging, and soon Tiger and Tom closed their eyes…

"Wakey, wakey," said a gentle, deep voice. The children stretched and opened their eyes. Grumps stood beside them.

"While we were in the land of nod, somebody has been in the pond."

The water had been stirred into brown clouds. The bubble-eyed frogs were gone and weeds were floating in clumps. The mud at the edge was thick and sticky. A brown path led from the pond to Grumps's kitchen door.

The kitchen floor was spattered with mud and Monday sat under the table, looking like a melted chocolate piglet.

"She must have followed you, Tiger," said Tom.

"I'm really sorry, Grumps. That's our warthog," said Tiger as she tried to grab Monday. "You are such a naughty wartie!"

At Tiger's cross voice, Monday squealed, dashed between them all and ran outside. Tiger raced after her just in time to see her dive and splat into the pond.

Monday wallowed and rolled and almost looked like she was smiling at the fact that nobody could reach her.

She did not want to come out.

Tiger and Tom squatted at the murky edge of the pond. When Monday waded closer, Tiger tried to pick her out of the muck, but she was slippery, like a brown bar of soap.

"Maybe we need a net," said Tom.

"I think she wants somebody to go in with her," said Grumps, laughing.

"Us?" said Tiger and Tom. "No way!"

Tiger went back to Willowgate to ask May Days what to do.

May Days was plumbing in a new

washing machine. She had oil on her hands, dust on her knees and piles of dirty laundry around her. Tiger told her what had happened.

"Warthogs love mud," May Days explained. "It's like sunscreen for a wartie."

"But we can't let her back in the house with all that mud on her," said Tiger.

"Good job you've made her a den outside then," said May Days. "Don't worry about that warthog. She'll come home when she's hungry."

Of course! Tiger raced back outside and banged the bucket from the other side of the hedge. Straightaway Monday slipped out of

the pond and dashed through the hedge to
see what was for dinner.

That night, Tiger was falling asleep when
the blanket over her sleeping bag slid
away. She tugged it back.

"Are you comfortable?" asked May Days.

"Something's pulling," said Tiger, and
the blanket whipped right off the bed.

May Days and Tiger crawled to the
ends of their camp beds to look.

There was Monday, holding the
blanket in her teeth. She wriggled,
commando-style, back through a hole
she'd dug under the pen. She dragged the

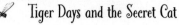

blanket behind her and stuffed it into her den, shuffling in after it.

"Maybe she was cold," said Tiger, leaning on her elbows.

"At least we know she can dig," May Days chuckled.

"May Days?" whispered Tiger, so as not to wake Monday.

"Yes?"

"Do you think Monday just wants to be near us?"

"Us?" said May Days. "I think she wants to be near you. Here," she said, reaching out and passing some more invisible Tiger Bravery, "you earned a whole lot more today."

Chapter 7

The Staring Oat

Monday had a den, so Tom thought they should have one too.

Tiger had her own bedroom at home and there was a corner of the playground at school that she and her friends liked to call their own, but she'd never had a den before.

"Could we call it our Holiday Den, Tom?" said Tiger.

"Tiger and Tom's Secret Holiday Den!" said Tom.

All they had to do was find somewhere to make it…

Tiger had only explored the smaller back garden around the tent and beech tree, and the hedge between Willowgate and Grumps's house.

"Where shall we start?" said Tom.

"This way," said Tiger, wondering what other secrets they might find in the rest of the garden. "We're going into the jungle."

They went around to the front of the house, past the leaning conservatory, wading through the long grass to the woodland at the side of the house.

It was a jungle of tall trees, swishing grasses, rustling brambles and wildlife scurrying away.

"Have you ever heard of the Staring Oat?" said Tom. The jungle was dense and they had to step high and push branches aside.

"What's the Staring Oat?" said Tiger, letting Tom go ahead.

"It lives in dark and dusty places, and scares the heebie-jeebies out of people."

"Where does the Staring Oat come from?" said Tiger.

"Nobody knows."

"Where is it now?"

"Nobody knows."

"What does it look like?" said Tiger, expecting Tom to say nobody knows again.

105

"It's got huge staring eyes," said Tom. "They're bright green, like giant glow-worms, and they spin, which makes you dizzy." He twirled and lurched around to show how giddy you might get. "And it's extremely frightening."

"How big is it?" said Tiger.

"Very big," said Tom. "And that –" he pointed and stopped spinning so Tiger bumped into him – "is just the kind of place you might find it."

Tiger's eyes followed Tom's pointing finger to an old shed. It was bigger than most garden sheds and the faded blue paint was cracked and creased. The hinges and handle were rusted, and cobwebs drooped from the dark windows.

"That is just the kind of place to be avoided," said Tiger, turning and heading back towards the safety of the house.

There, they found that Monday had dug another hole under the pen and escaped again. Their den would have to wait.

Tiger and Tom looked around the tent, and then in all the rooms and cupboards of the house. Holly the cat sat by the window in one of the bedrooms, staring into the garden.

"Holly, have you seen Monday?" said Tiger. The cat looked over at Tiger, just for a moment. Her tail flowed from the windowsill, down in a straight line, before curving back up slowly, like a hook. "I see you're busy fishing with your tail," said Tiger.

They checked Grumps's pond, but there was no tell-tale swirling swamp to say that

Monday had been there.

"We've looked in all the usual places," said Tiger, anxious that Monday might have gone to look for her as she had done before.

May Days gave Tiger a hug and patted the pocket where she kept her Tiger Bravery.

"I am trying to be brave," whispered Tiger in May Days' ear, but she was finding it hard when worry whirled in her tummy. Where was that wartie?

Some of the floorboards were loose from the plumbing work, so May Days went to check that Monday hadn't fallen down a hole somewhere.

Tiger and Tom searched the front garden. They ran under the trailing branches of the willow tree that sprawled across the lawn, but Monday wasn't there. They tramped through the long grass, they searched in the brambles, and they checked under the shrubs. No sign of the missing wartie.

"We've looked everywhere," said Tiger, caring very much what might have happened to the little warthog.

And then Holly came sauntering past. She looked over her shoulder, kinked her tail into a question-mark shape and seemed to be asking the children to follow.

She led them deep into the jungle garden, along the path they had flattened earlier, towards... the Staring Oat Shed.

"Just because it's the scariest looking place, with the biggest cobwebs and the darkest space, it doesn't mean she's in here," wailed Tiger. But by now they'd searched everywhere else.

"Who's going in to find out?" said Tom.

Tiger hadn't wanted the wartie to stay at Willowgate at first, but now she couldn't think of anything else except how much she missed Monday and wanted her to be safe.

"We're going to go in the Staring Oat Shed," said Tiger, "but first we need to be prepared."

Wearing a hard hat and visor, Tom batted and flattened a wide path through the jungle, using an old wooden tennis racket, until they were close to the treacherous shed.

"What's the mirror for?" whispered Tiger, crouched behind him, wearing yellow rubber gloves.

Tom had brought Grumps's shaving mirror.

"It will reflect the sun and shine a bright light in the Staring Oat's eyes," whispered Tom, "and while it's blinded, we can go in and get Monday." He looked at what Tiger was holding. "What's the hosepipe for?"

"Squirting."

"On the count of three…" said Tom.

"I've got the jitters and the creeps, Tom," said Tiger. But she thought about Monday, who might be trapped in the shed feeling even more scared than *she* was. Tiger took a deep breath.

Tom was very quiet for a moment. He had a key ring in his pocket. Hanging on the end was a small plum-shaped ball of green fluff, with two googly eyes and flat, felt feet.

"I don't think that is going to scare the

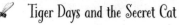

Staring Oat," said Tiger.

"It's my gonk," said Tom. "It's for making you smile when you're glum."

Tiger smiled, but her tummy was in turmoil. Poor Monday. Would the Staring Oat let her go?

"It helps if you've got something in your pocket," said Tom, putting the gonk back in his. "Especially when you're scared."

Tiger put her hand in her pocket. Tiger Bravery was invisible, it couldn't be touched or felt, but she knew it was there.

She might have just enough to face the Staring Oat and rescue Monday.

"Ready now?" said Tom, and Tiger

gulped and nodded. "On the count of three…"

"Can we do the count of twenty?" said Tiger, which they did, counting slowly, until Tom shouted,

"Twenty!
Charge!"

Tom slammed the door open, waving his racket.

Monday was there! Shivering and quivering.

And what else was that?

Tom caught the light on the mirror and flashed it around.

Tiger turned on the
hosepipe and only a trickle
of water dribbled out
because the perilous
plumbing was still
up the spout. She
dropped the hose while

Tom swung his racket. Tiger scooped up Monday and ran back out with the piglet under her arm, pulling Tom behind her. They burst out of the shed, past Holly, who was sitting calmly, licking her paw.

"Did you see the Staring Oat?" said Tom, panting.

"It was huge," said Tiger. "Like a big gonk, but not hairy or funny."

"We were lucky it was lying down asleep and we didn't have to stare into its eyes," said Tom.

Tiger held the trembling wartie in her arms. "Poor Monday, stuck in the Staring Oat Shed," said Tiger. "You are to stay right by my side from now on. Got it?"

 117

Tom made a sign from a stick and a piece of cardboard.

WARNING: STARING OAT!
PEOPLE KEEP OUT!
AND THAT MEANS WARTHOGS
TOO!

They thought about adding Holly's name, but that cat didn't seem scared of anything.

"I'm going to dazzle the Staring Oat and slay it, and then the shed will be ours," said Tom.

"Please can we do it another time?"

said Tiger. "Monday is still scared out of her wits."

That night, Tiger lay at the wrong end of her camp bed, with her head sticking out of the tent, watching Monday, who was safe in the den, wrapped in her blanket. And just as Tiger was wondering if Holly had led them to the shed on purpose, that white cat came wandering over.

Holly looked through the wire at the wartie and, with one light spring, bounced over the side of the pen.

As if she knew that Monday hated to be alone, she curled up beside her.

"Well, Holly," whispered Tiger, "you look like you missed Monday today too."

Chapter 8

Do You Love Warthogs Yet?

Monday was in her pen, happily snuffling around in the soil. She had begun to eats roots and grass and other things in the earth. Holly sat nearby in the sun, blinking sleepily, so Tiger crawled through the hedge to see Tom.

Grumps was making a cake and Tom stood on a chair beside him, watching the whisking food processor.

"What's your favourite animal?" Tiger asked Tom.

"Guinea pig," he said.

"Have you got a guinea pig?"

"No, I'm not even allowed a pet spider at home."

"Have you ever even held a guinea pig?" said Tiger.

"Once," said Tom. "My friend Jeremy Costa has one."

Grumps scraped the cake mixture into tins while Tom licked the whisk.

"What's your favourite animal, Grumps?" asked Tiger.

"Well, now…" He scratched his head and thought for a moment. "I like bears,"

he said. "Brown bears and teddy bears."
Grumps grinned.

Bears were nice, thought Tiger, but
they weren't tigers.

Grumps leaned in to Tiger and
whispered, "I had a special teddy bear
called Rhubarb when I was a boy." He
winked. "I used to carry him everywhere
to make me feel brave."

"Do you still have Rhubarb?" asked
Tiger, touching her pocket of Tiger
Bravery.

Grumps smiled. "He's in the attic,
because I seem to be able to manage
without him most of the time now."

The cake went in the oven, just as

Tiger heard a horn honking over at Willowgate.

Dennis had arrived with his van and, with Tom busy curling his tongue around a wooden spoon, Tiger ran down to open the gate.

"What's your favourite animal, Dennis?" asked Tiger.

"I used to like pelicans," he said, "but I prefer elephants now. Less pecky."

Dennis had come to check on Monday, so Tiger helped put her in a box on the weighing scales.

Monday had reached her target weight.

"Well done, Monday," said Tiger, holding her a little bit longer than she needed to. "I knew you could do it." She kissed her on her snout, which made Monday grunt softly.

"Does this mean she's finished growing?" asked Tiger.

"No, there's still a way to go," said Dennis, "but she looks ready for the next phase of Operation Wartie."

"Ooh, did you hear that, Monday?" Tiger scratched the bristly wartie just behind the ears. "I'll go and get Tom. He has been a very brave animal trainer and he'll want to know what our plan is."

Dennis bit the corner of his lip. He took

off his sunglasses. His eyes were usually bright and sparkling, but there was a sadness in them today. He crouched down beside Tiger.

"The next phase is for Monday to be introduced to a new family of warthogs. I've come to collect her and take her back to the zoo today," said Dennis gently. "You'd better get Tom to come and say goodbye."

Nobody had told Tiger that Monday had to go back. It wouldn't have mattered in the beginning, but it mattered terribly now.

"Monday's not ready," cried Tiger. "She isn't brave enough yet."

Tiger ran to the tent with Monday under her arm. She zipped up the flappy door to keep everyone out. She pulled her sleeping bag under the camp bed and made a den for her and Monday to hide in.

A little while later, Tiger heard someone walking towards the tent. "Tiger," called May Days, "come out for a cuddle."

"I'm not coming out," sniffed Tiger. "And neither is Monday. She needs me."

Tiger heard more footsteps. "Tiger?" said Tom. "Can I come in?"

"No," said Tiger. "Monday is asleep and doesn't want to be disturbed. Ever again!"

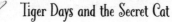

It went quiet for a while.

There was rustling and whispering
and things moved about outside the tent,
making noises that Tiger didn't recognise.
She unzipped the flap a little and she and
Monday poked their noses out to see what
was going on. Holly was sitting there, right

by the tent, watching too.

May Days and Dennis, Tom and
Grumps, had pulled up a picnic table and
chairs outside. They had a teapot and
mugs, and a fat vanilla sponge decorated
with stripes of apricot jam and cream, so it
looked a little tiger-ish.

Tiger zipped the tent door back up. They could all stay out there for the rest of the week eating cake, Monday was not going back to the zoo. She would be lonely and scared without Tiger to look after her. But Tiger couldn't help listening when the conversation was all about her favourite subject.

"There's a magician in America who makes tigers appear," said Tom. "Grumps saw it for real."

"Where do the tigers come from?" said May Days.

"I don't know – they're magic!" said Tom.

May Days laughed.

"We had a Bengal tiger at the zoo

once. She was fiercely protective of her cubs," said Dennis.

"Tigers were my favourite animal when I was a girl," said May Days, and Tiger sat up. She still held Monday in her arms, but wished she was outside on her grandmother's lap, just as much as she wished for Monday to stay at Willowgate.

From inside the tent, Tiger said, "Were they really?"

Tom, Grumps and Dennis tiptoed away quietly.

"Did I tell you about that time when I was a girl and my parents lived in India?" said May Days. "I was at boarding school in England, which made living with wildlife a piece of cake."

Tiger leaned over and pressed her ear against the tent door.

"During the school holidays I would go and stay with my parents," continued May Days. "One day, I was wandering around the garden. It was a beautiful garden, some of it landscaped, and some overgrown and jungle-like—"

"Like Willowgate?" said Tiger through the canvas.

"Very much like Willowgate," said May Days. "Perhaps even wilder."

"And?" said Tiger.

"And one day, as I wandered around," said May Days, "you will never guess what I came face to face with."

"A tiger?" gasped Tiger. She had never heard anything so spellbinding.

"Yes, a real tiger. The most beautiful creature I had ever seen. Can you imagine how that felt?" said May Days.

Tiger nodded, shook her head, nodded again. "I don't know, but you must have been scared," she said, unzipping the tent.

"Yes, at first, because she looked me right in the eye to show me how mighty and brave she was," said May Days, opening her arms wide. Tiger came out of the tent, still holding Monday, and climbed on to her grandmother's lap.

"You remind me of that tiger," said May Days. "How brave and strong you have been to take care of that little wartie."

"What happened with the tiger?" said Tiger.

"She turned and walked away," said May Days. "I have loved and respected all animals since, their strengths and their weaknesses, which make them what they are."

Tiger curled into May Days.

"It's so hard to choose my favourite animal at the moment," said Tiger, holding Monday tight.

"You are allowed to love as many creatures as you like," said May Days. "But the biggest thing an animal trainer has to learn, is to let them go when it's time."

Tiger touched her pocket of Tiger Bravery. She had more than enough now.

Dennis walked back from the kitchen and smiled at Tiger.

"I love Monday," she said, finally handing over the little warthog.

"I know," said May Days.

"Be brave, Monday," said Tiger, giving her handfuls of invisible Warthog Bravery. "You'll make new warthog friends at the zoo and I promise to come and visit you." She would miss the naughty, adorable wartie so very badly, but Tiger knew she had to let her go.

"I saw another real tiger today," said May Days. "Perhaps the bravest I ever saw."

"Where?" said Tiger. "Is there one here at Willowgate?"

"Yes," said May Days. "And I hope she will come and visit me all the time now."

Mr Days arrived to collect Tiger and drive her home. Tiger showed her dad the tent where she'd been sleeping and pointed out the scary Staring Oat Shed and warned him to keep well away. Tiger wanted her dad to meet Holly, but couldn't find her anywhere…

Finally, it was time to say goodbye and as they drove away from Willowgate House, Tiger waved and waved through the rear window to May Days, Tom Henry Thomas and Grumps.

"Did you enjoy your adventure at Willowgate?" said Mr Days.

"It was very skew-whiff," said Tiger. "But I didn't mind at all."

Holly was sitting by the gate as they left, her tail curling gently as if she was also beckoning Tiger to come back another day. Tiger had a feeling that the cat would be there when she returned. Her tummy fluttered a little as she wondered, who else might be visiting Willowgate the next time she came?

Join Tiger Days on her next adventure...

TIGER DAYS

and the Moonlight Foxes

When Tiger returns to Willowgate House
a new adventure begins.

Holly the cat is nowhere to be found and
objects keep going missing. Tiger and Tom
have a mystery to uncover as they
become... Pet Detectives!

Out 25th August 2016